chengdu

COULD not, WOULD not fall asleep

Written and illustrated by
BARNEY SALTZBERG

Disney • HYPERION BOOKS

NEW YORK

Copyright © 2014 by Barney Saltzberg
Published by Disney · Hyperion Books,
an imprint of Disney Book Group.

For information address Disney · Hyperion Books, 125 West End Avenue, New York, New York 10023.

Printed in Malaysia

First Edition

1 3 5 7 9 10 8 6 4 2
H106-9333-5-13349
Library of Congress Cataloging-in-Publication Data
Saltzberg, Barney, author, illustrator.
Chengdu could not, would not fall asleep / written and illustrated by Barney Saltzberg.—First edition.
pages cm
Summary: High in the trees in the middle of the night, all of the pandas are sleeping
except for Chengdu, who tries everything and still cannot fall asleep until he finds
the perfect spot—atop his brother, Yuan.
ISBN 978-1-4231-6721-1 (hardback)
[1. Sleep—Fiction. 2. Pandas—Fiction. 3. Bedtime—Fiction.] I. Title.
PZ7.S1552Che 2014
[E]—dc23   2013029121

Reinforced binding

Visit www.disneyhyperionbooks.com

For my adventurous wife, Susan,
whose incredible photographs inspired this book.
If I were Chengdu, you would be my Yuan

-B.S.

It was late,
and it was quiet,

and everyone in
the bamboo grove
was sleeping . . .

everyone
except . . .

Chengdu.

No matter what
Chengdu tried,
he could not,
would not
fall asleep.

Chengdu turned

and he tossed

but he
could not,
would not
fall asleep.

and he twitched,

Chengdu scrunched

but he still could not,
would not fall asleep.

and he rolled

and he hung upside down,

Chengdu was
very tired.
He really
wanted to
be sleeping.

So he
climbed
up . . .

and up

and up,

until he found
the perfect
spot.

And soon
everyone in the
bamboo grove
was sleeping . . .

everyone except . . .

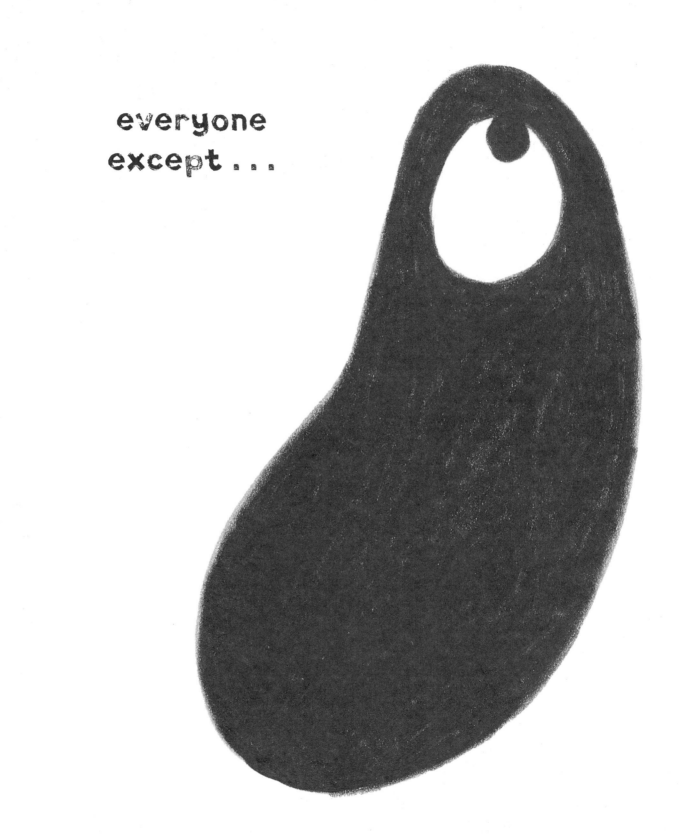

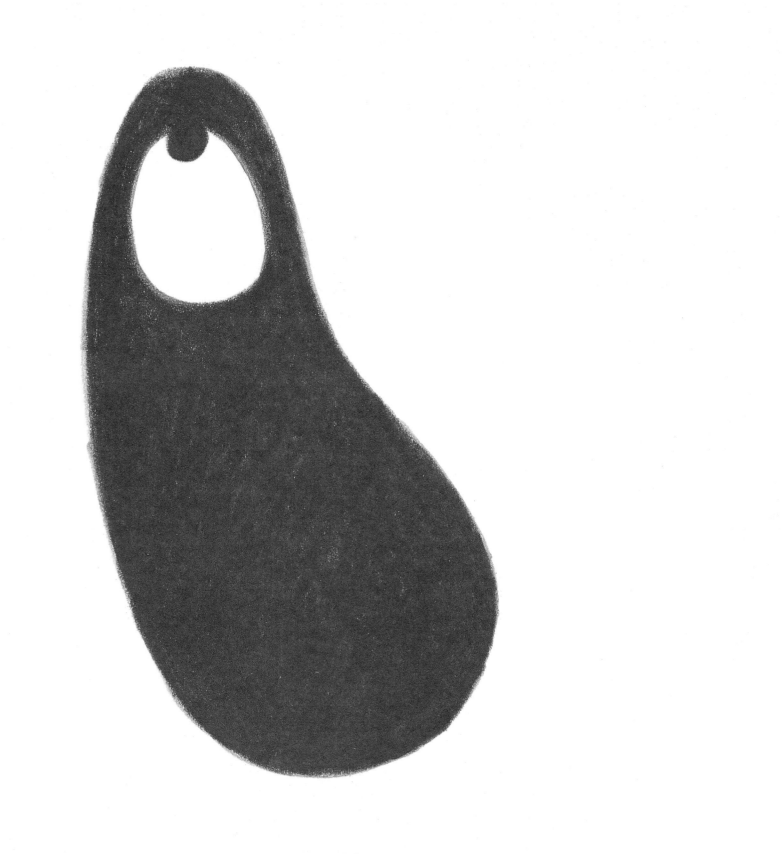

Chengdu's
brother, Yuan.